Meg's World

Written & Illustrated
by
John Kollock

The Saturday Shop

Clarkesville, Georgia

The Saturday Shop
P.O. Box 315
Clarkesville, GA 30523

Manufactured in the United States

Revised Edition
6th Printing
1996

ISBN 0-9613242-1-X

One day Meg came dancing into the room on happy bare feet. Impulsively she hugged my arm and gave it a fierce warm smack with her lips.

"I kiss the world, because God made it," she said joyfully, in what seemed to me the most wholehearted endorsement of this planet that I have ever heard.

Then with a bound she was off to some new adventure around the corner and down the hall. I sat there thinking that here was a young lady of four and a little bit, who was looking at our tired old surroundings with the fresh new eyes of youth that seemed to see things a lot clearer than those which had been looking for a lot longer.

I began to listen more carefully to what she reported and observed. There was a twist to it that sounded truer than the real thing — as if she had cocked her mind jauntily over one eye. This was the world of someone who had not yet been exposed to the learning process—the discipline of facts — A+ and D−.

It would not last. In a year she would have to succumb to the ritual of education and the criticism of her fellow students. But while it was still springing forth, full of the confidence of innocent enthusiasm, for that precious little time — this was Meg's World.

J.C.K.
Misty Valley, 1970

To Meg herself, and the people in her world

My name is Meg, and this is Monday. This is my room — all the way over to Kathleen's bed.

My sisters are getting ready to go to school. I don't go to school because I am only this many fingers. Next year I will be a whole handful. Mother says I am one now. I guess she can't count.

We are always very busy on Monday. The girls have to find their school clothes, and their books, and shoes and socks to match. Sometimes I help – sometimes I just watch.

We have a cat named Cricket. He doesn't go to school either. Cats are born smart. I was born smart too, but I have forgotten some things, like reading and counting up. I know what 4 and 7 and 10 look like, because that is how much we girls are. Mother is a hundred, I think. Daddy says he feels like a million, but I don't think he is that many. Maybe only four or three hundred.

When the girls have gone to school, I have to go to work. I help my Mother with the house. This is really why I don't go to school, because I am so busy all day.

On Mondays we clean.

I like to clean, especially with the vacuum cleaner. It will eat almost anything I feed it. Once I tried to feed it Cricket. Vacuum cleaners don't eat cats. Not all the way down anyway.

Cricket eats cat food. I feed it to him sometimes when he doesn't eat all of it. It's good for him.

Cricket has a bad leg that got under a car when it wooshed by. Everyone said he was squished flat, but he only sits funny now. We have had Cricket since he was a tiny kitty. I carry him around when he gets tired of walking, even if I have to catch him under the bed to do it.

There are lots of ways to carry a cat, because they bend so easily.

When the girls have gone to school I get
lonesome once in a while. Then I get all of the
dolls — mine and Carey's and Kathleen's — and
we have a together party. Then I feel better.

Some days I have company come over to visit.

Company does not always want to play what you want them to. Last week I wanted to play gorilla, but Mary wanted to be a fairy tale. You can't always have your own way, even if you yell. ·

We get the costumes from the big box at the foot of my bed.

When you play "dress up" the company always gets to be the princess or the fairy. This is called manners.

I get to be the boy — or the gorilla when they will play it.

After "dress up" we get out some more toys. Sometimes we remember to put-each-thing-back-in-its-place-when-we-have-finished-playing-with-it.

Sometimes we forget.

We also play in the yard. I like to play spider. We run all over the yard with string and weave our web. Mary says that spiders catch their dinner in the web.

All we ever catch is Mother and the postman. You can't eat postmen. They belong to the government, like police and the garbage man.

When company comes we get to have juice
and cookies. Tea parties are so much more fun
than lunch.

Then we listen to records and I tell Mary that I am going to California to visit my friends on the records. I will too. Last week I almost went, but it was raining. I think California is out beyond the grocery store.

I may need a map.

On Tuesdays Mother goes to make Kathleen and her friends into Bluebirds. After you get to be a Bluebird, then you get to be a Campfire. Then you get to be a Mother or a Grandmother or somebody's Aunt.

On Tuesdays I go to visit my Nana. Nanas are nice. They never have anything to do but play. We play cards, and puzzles, and walk in her garden. The only bad thing about Nanas is they don't sit down on the floor very well.

And they are too big for playhouses and hidy-holes.

I have hidy-holes under the bushes at our house. No one can see me, and I can see them back.

When I get very big I am going to live in one of my hidy-holes. My husband will live there too. I hope he likes acorns. I also hope he fits. My Daddy doesn't. But he is not a husband—he is a Daddy and they are bigger. Thomas can get into my hidy-hole if I let him.

But he is no fun, and he won't eat acorns.

Sometimes there are boxes.

Things come in them, but that doesn't matter. When they get out, we get the boxes. Next to hidy-holes I love boxes best. When they are new they smell funny and clean. They are dark inside and you sound big when you yell.

If Mother makes some holes you can have a house, or a ship, or a TV show. Then when you get too many friends inside you can still use the box for a sled, or a new rug in your hidy-hole.

Boxes almost never wear out, unless it rains.

Wednesday is nothing. I am not even sure there is one every week. Nothing ever happens on Wednesday, because it is so close to Thursday and that is when we go shopping. I hope someday they will invent something for Wednesday to be. Maybe a long nap.

HEALTH AIDS · HOUSEWARE

On Thursday we go shopping at the store.

This is a very busy day. We have lots of things to buy. Food and candy and cookies and jelly beans and chocolate balls and like that. The girls and Daddy eat a lot. I don't eat very much, just teenie candy and teenie cookies and lots and lots of tennie chewing gum.

Mother always takes a list to the store to remember with. I don't need a list — I can always remember what I want.

Sometimes we look at dresses and material and hats.

I look beautiful in hats.

Mother looks tired.

I also help with getting lunch. Mother is very old and can't do much. I have to stay busy to keep her interested in things.

Sometimes Mother takes exercise with the people on TV to keep her tummy flat. It pokes out a lot. Mine does too.

The people on TV don't have fat tummies. I don't know why they exercise, except to keep Mother company.

After lunch I usually take a little rest, because my Humpty gets lonesome for me.

When I get up Mother is always talking on
the phone. Phones are not fun, unless I am
talking to Nana.

I usually do a little rearranging while Mother
is talking. She is always surprised at how much
I can do.

If the housework is done early, I might go visit my friend Baby Laura. She is a very tiny baby. I think she is not even one year old yet. That means she is zero — no fingers. She wants to talk, but no one will tell her how.

I like babies. At Christmas everyone talks about the Baby Jesus, but we never play with him. I think maybe he has a cold.

Christmas comes near winter — I know because you can't go swimming. Sometimes it snows and that is winter too. Summer is when we visit our cousins on the farm. The rest of the time is just weather — except Easter and Halloween.

On Easter I am very clean and there are candy eggs under the sofa. Daddy puts them there because he is the Easter Bunny.

Halloween is Mr. Pete. He doesn't know it's me when I "trick or treat" him. Even when I say "Hey, I'm Meg," he just laughs and gives me more candy. I wish Mr. Pete was the Easter Bunny too.

Friday is a happy day. The girls are out of school for the weekend, and there is lots of playing to do.

We play in the yard on Friday. There is a little tree the girls call the "climbing tree." We all learned to climb on it, and swing on it, and exercise on it. But with all that exercise, it still doesn't grow.

So I water it a lot.

While the girls do their homework, I help Mother cook supper.

When I cook I like to try new dishes—and new cups and spoons. Biscuits are fun to make. Even if you drop them, they don't break. Eggs are no fun — they can get you into big trouble.

I like to play with salt. It feels like tiny sand but it tastes better.

The thing I like best about cooking is washing dishes. Mother must like it too because she always washes them again when I get through.

When we start cooking supper Daddy smells it and comes home. I don't know where he goes all day, but he doesn't get very dirty.

Daddy is very old and tired. If he lies down I sit on him to make him comfortable. Pretty soon he gets up because he isn't very tired any more.

At supper we say Grace. That is when you put your head down near your plate and peek between your fingers at the food. Everyone takes turns thanking God for supper, even if he didn't cook it. I can say Grace the fastest.

After supper on Friday we all watch TV. Daddy says it is hard to concentrate. That is because he is so restless. We watch till it is time for bed. We have to get lots of rest because the next day is Saturday.

Saturday is like summer. Then you have fun and everyone is home. All but Daddy — he comes and goes. In the summer we go to the farm to visit our cousins. On Saturdays we go to the store to spend the girls' allowance.

It is very hard to spend an allowance. There is so much to want and next Saturday is a long way off. Many things you want are only for Christmas and Birthdays. Usually the girls just get candy. Sometimes it is so hard to decide they just save their money in their banks.

When I get an allowance I will make up my mind quick. I have already decided on everything I will buy until I am twenty years old. Then I will get married and have to buy only food and dress material.

Carey is rich. Her teeth are always falling out and she has this fairy who comes around at night and pays her money for them. Sometimes she leaves a note and says don't take the teeth, and the dumb fairy doesn't even take what he is paying for. I don't really believe in fairies — but if I ever lose a tooth I will.

If it rains we play in our rooms or under the tables. Then everyone builds a house for her doll.

We wash hair on Saturday night. Then we wash all over. I brush my teeth very well on Saturday night, because God comes on Sunday.

Sunday is Sunday School. This is the only school I go to. It makes me itch. Every time I have to sit still and not talk I itch.

We say Grace a lot at Sunday School, but there isn't any food with it.

We also sing. I like to sing, especially when I am dancing. They don't want you to dance while you sing at Sunday School. I think the teacher would like to anyway.

They tell us all about God. God makes us all
different. That's just the way it is. He doesn't
do it to be mean. He makes some people fat.
Candy can make you fat, too. But God doesn't
care. He just wants you to be good and not
talk about people who are fat.

We also color and glue at Sunday School.
After that we say Grace some more, and my
fingers smell funny.

Sometimes we eat out for lunch on Sunday. I like to eat where the chairs go round and round and they have lots of onions and catsup. Catsup will wash out if you don't get too much on you. You should never spin around and try to eat with lots of catsup, because there are always fat ladies nearby who get excited. Ice cream will also drip if you eat a hole in the bottom first.

Sunday afternoon we go to see people who are still clean from Church. Usually they are people we don't see any other time. I do not know if they are clean on Tuesday. When we get dirty enough, we go home and maybe watch TV or read.

Mother reads the best. Daddy reads with funny voices and waves his arms a lot. It's hard to go to sleep when Daddy reads. Sometimes we read about the Bible on Sunday. God sees everything we do and hears everything we say — if the windows are open.

We wash again on Sunday night. This is because you can't take germs to school on Monday. Carey has the most germs because she is the biggest. Sometimes when she is mad she calls me names like 'Air Pollution.' If I can't think what to call her back I just tell Mother on her. I wish I knew more big bad words.

On my next birthday I will be five. Then I won't cry any more or suck my fingers, and I can get married or go to Kindergarten. The girls say you have to sit still in school — all day long. I'm not sure I want to go to school. Mother says I have to go — to learn to be something.

But I'm already something — I'm Meg.

That's all—Amen—Goodnight.

JOHN KOLLOCK has illustrated over 30 books for other authors in addition to six of his own creation. These include *Think Persian*, *The Not So Empty Nest*, *The Long Afternoon*, *These Gentle Hills*, *Seasons of Light*, and *Meg's World*, which is now in its sixth printing. John is also well known in his region of North Georgia for having created over 60 limited edition prints depicting the rural history and life in this area. He and his wife Nancy live on the family farm which is the setting for several of his books.

For additional copies of *Meg's World*, write to:

The Saturday Shop
P.O. Box 315
Clarkesville, GA 30523